THE
SEVEN
LADY GODIVAS

THE
SEVEN
LADY GODIVAS

WRITTEN AND ILLUSTRATED BY

Dr. Seuss

PUBLISHED BY
RANDOM HOUSE
NEW YORK

Copyright 1939 by Dr. Seuss. Copyright renewed 1967 by Dr.
Seuss. All rights reserved under International and Pan-American
Copyright Conventions. Published in the United States by
Random House, Inc., New York, and simultaneously in Canada
by Random House of Canada Limited, Toronto.

Library of Congress Cataloging-in-Publication Data:

Seuss, Dr.   The seven Lady Godivas.
I. Title.   PS3513.E2S4   1987   813'.52   86-31541
ISBN: 0-394-56269-0 (trade); 0-394-56779-X (ltd. ed.)
Manufactured in the United States of America
1 2 3 4 5 6 7 8 9 0
First printing of the reissued edition, September 1987

To
Lady Clementina Godiva
Lady Dorcas J. Godiva
Lady Arabella Godiva
Lady Mitzi Godiva
Lady Lulu Godiva
Lady Gussie Godiva
Lady Hedwig Godiva
this historical document is admiringly dedicated.

Foreword

HISTORY has treated no name so shabbily as it has the name Godiva.

Today Lady Godiva brings to mind a shameful picture—a big blond nude trotting around the town on a horse. In the background of this picture, there is always Peeping Tom, an illicit snooper with questionable intentions.

The author feels that the time has come to speak:

> *There was not one; there were Seven Lady Godivas, and their nakedness actually was not a thing of shame. So far as Peeping Tom is concerned, he never really peeped. "Peeping" was merely the old family name, and Tom and his six brothers bore it with pride.*

A beautiful story of love, honor and scientific achievement has too long been gathering dust in the archives.

Dr. Seuss
Coventry, 1939

THE
SEVEN
LADY GODIVAS

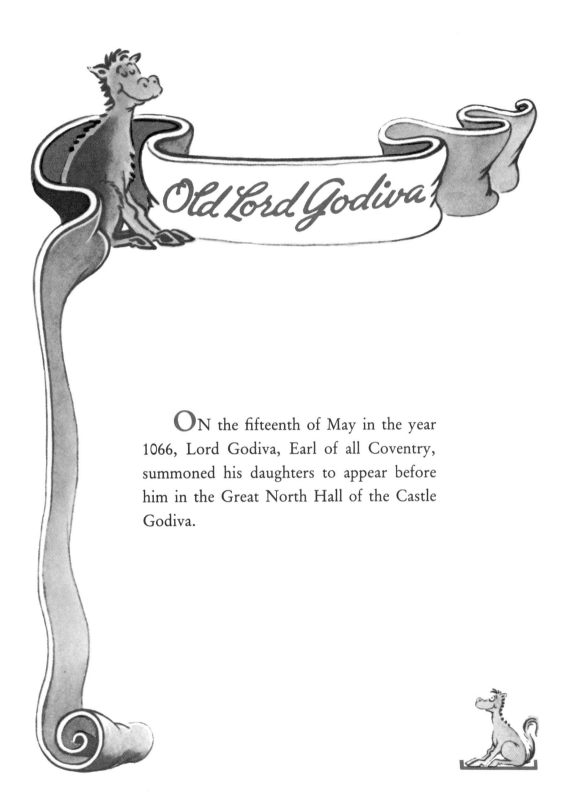

Old Lord Godiva

ON the fifteenth of May in the year 1066, Lord Godiva, Earl of all Coventry, summoned his daughters to appear before him in the Great North Hall of the Castle Godiva.

For a long silent moment he regarded them proudly, for the seven daughters of Lord Godiva had brains. Nowhere, he thought with satisfaction, could there be a group of young ladies that wasted less time upon frivol and froth. No fluffy-duff primping, no feather, no fuss. They were simply themselves and chose not to disguise it.

"Girls," announced Lord Godiva, "today I leave for the Battle of Hastings. And," he added calmly, "I'm going by horseback."

Horseback!

The sisters looked nervously from one to another. In that day in England, the horse was not taken lightly. True, Lord Godiva had been experimenting with these animals for years. But the horse remained a mystery, unbroken in spirit, a contrary beast full of wiles and surprises.

"Come, come," chided Lord Godiva, rattling his spurs. "Don't be so old-fashioned. This is 1066! Definitely, I shall attend the battle on horseback."

Lord Godiva had spoken. His metal feet clanked as he led his daughters to the courtyard. Their bare feet followed, cold on the cobbles.

Waiting and saddled stood Nathan, his war horse. From the eyeholes in his hoodgear, he watched the group approaching.

"Nice horse," smiled Lord Godiva, holding out a lump of sugar. Nathan ignored it; he looked sullen and foreboding. Lord Godiva put the sugar back in the pocket of his armor.

He climbed into the saddle and aimed for the drawbridge. Nathan started off in a sidewise sort of trot.

"Good luck!" shouted the girls, waving their handkerchiefs.

"To victory!" shouted Lord Godiva, brandishing his broadsword.

But everyone must have shouted too loud.

Nathan reared. His front knees dipped low and his hind knees flew high, and he pitched Lord Godiva, Earl of all Coventry, spurs over breastplate, off on his helm.

By the time his daughters reached him, the old warrior was dead. Like any normal daughters, the Godiva Sisters wept.

Then they stiffened their shoulders and faced the facts. Their father was gone, destroyed by a horse! The girls were left with a grim obligation.

Horses must be studied and charted, made safe for posterity.

Seven hands clasped over Lord Godiva's remains. Seven tongues spoke. Seven pledges were uttered.

"I swear," swore each, "that I shall not wed until I have brought to the light of this world some new and worthy Horse Truth, of benefit to man."

It was an oath of heroic proportions. How long this Horse Truth Quest might take was something no Godiva knew. But each one knew she was sad and sick at heart. Each one was in love, each one betrothed.

That night, when the seven Peeping Brothers came to court their ladies, all doors of the Castle Godiva were bolted. Nailed to every door was a copy of the oath.

Very sadly, Peeping Tom, Peeping Dick, Peeping Harry, Peeping Jack, Peeping Drexel, Peeping Sylvester and Peeping Frelinghuysen each dropped his bouquet into the moat.

Then they all went home to wait.

"Teenie" Godiva

THE next morning Hedwig awoke in the chill of the dawn.

"I am the eldest," she thought, as she brushed her teeth. "I must manage these oaths in a systematic way."

She cut sheets of parchment and stitched them together. She bound them with care in a cover of rawhide. To the top of this volume she hitched a bronze chain. Then she knocked at her sisters' doors.

"Follow me," said Hedwig. Just that and nothing more. Six solemn Godivas followed Hedwig to the stables.

Hedwig hung the volume just outside the stable door. Then she showed them the contents—exactly seven pages, and each one a blank.

"Somewhere there are Horse Truths," Hedwig said briefly. "Each of us must find one and inscribe it on her page.

"An oath has been sworn. That oath shall be kept. *So long as your page remains empty of Horse Truth, so shall your life remain empty of love.*"

A terrible silence filled the stable courtyard. The mind of each Godiva was far away with her Peeping. . . .

Hedwig stamped her foot. "Enough of this wishy-washy schoolgirl mooning! *To horse!*" she shouted and plunged into the barn.

A clatter of hoofbeats rang through the yard. Over the drawbridge they made for the fields. Through the fens and the bracken, through thistle and gorse, through moorland and marshland. The great Quest was on!

But Teenie Godiva was not with the others. Left behind, left alone, left unnoticed . . . Teenie was too fat for any horse to carry.

She sat down on a small pile of oats and wept. Her prospects added up badly indeed. "No horse, no Horse Truth. No Horse Truth, no Peeping. No Peeping, no nothing."

By and by the oats became very uncomfortable. Teenie got up and went into the stable.

Dejected, she wandered past stall after stall. Out in the sunlight her sisters were trotting, galloping, cantering, earning their love-right. . . .

Here it was hot and the horses dozed drearily.

"No co-operation," she sighed, as she trudged down the aisles.

At Teenie's elbow a lazy mare yawned. An enormous crude yawn, uncouth and ill mannered. Teenie stalked on. Then she sensed something strange, and she stopped and looked back.

The yawn, to her amazement, was still going on. Wider and wider the beast's jaws stretched open. The yawn of all yawns, it blossomed; it bloomed from gap stage to gape stage, from gape stage to gawp. At last it reached its zenith and froze there, ajar.

Teenie had never seen anything like it.

"I say," puzzled Teenie, "maybe this isn't a yawn after all."

The horse almost seemed to be inviting inspection.

She stepped up to the mare. It stood still and obliging. She stepped up quite close and she peered down its windpipe.

When her sisters returned to the castle for lunch, they found Teenie in bed. From the crown of her head to the scruff of her neck, she was swathed deep in bandages, ointment and lint.

"Nose gone," she said simply.

"Teenie! Poor Teenie!" gasped her horrified sisters.

"Poor Teenie nothing!" A radiant smile filtered up through the gauze. "You know that mare Uncle Ethelbert gave us last Christmas? With the help of the darling, I've filled in my page."

"A Horse Truth?"

"A great one," said Teenie. *"Don't ever look a gift horse in the mouth!"*

In spite of the fact she was in no shape for kissing, Teenie Godiva married Peeping Tom that very night.

In spite of the fact she was in no shape for kissing, Teenie Godiva married Peeping Tom that very night.

IN their bachelor household, next morning, the Peepings were in high hopeful spirits. A Horse Truth had been consummated on the very first day!

"At this rate," rejoiced the brothers, "we'll all be married within the week."

And at breakfast in the castle, Arabella, Mitzi, Lulu, Gussie and Hedwig Godiva simply bubbled with cheer. The Horse Truth Quest was going to be easy.

But Dorcas J. Godiva sat cool and unemotional.

"It was a fluke, girls," she declared. "Teenie was just plain lucky. And if you're planning to loaf around the barns and let the horses do the thinking, I warn you, girls, right here and now, you'll never win your Peepings. *Research*, believe me, is our one and only answer."

"What's research?" Lulu, puzzled, looked up from her herring.

"Research," explained Dorcas, "is the concentrated examination and correlation of the multitudinous phenomena co-existent in some specific field of activity. For my field I have selected the study of Horse-Drawn Vehicular Transportation."

Her sisters were not interested. Leaving them to loll and lounge in the stables, waiting for Horse Truths to drop in their laps, the analytical Godiva plunged into her research.

In buggies and tumbrils, in sulkies and shays, she rumbled through the highways and byways of Coventry. Each day a different vehicle, each day the selfsame horse, and she watched his every action with a sharp and eager eye.

But Thidwick, her horse, was a hard nut to crack. Stolid and placid, he pulled without emotion. His Truths, if he had such, he kept to himself.

"My wagons," thought Dorcas, "must be made more provoking." Thidwick was smug and he needed a jolt.

So she rigged up a gig she called "Wagon *Superior*." She constructed the wagon part purposely low, so that every fourth step, when his hind quarters rose, the boards slapped a rhythmic tattoo on his rump.

Dorcas was right. Thidwick's smugness was visibly shaken. In his eyes she detected a flicker of protest.

She determined to pique him a little bit more. . . .

She rigged up a gig she called "Wagon *Inferior*." Thidwick objected with ill humor and scorn. He had just about become accustomed to the wagon up on top, and *now* the wretched woman had slung one down below, down between his knees, so he had to trot wide, in a disgraceful, undignified, bowlegged gait.

His mood, at the end of the day, was just foul.

Dorcas was elated. In the smoldering depths of his mounting distemper, something was brewing—and it might be a Horse Truth!

So she went a step further.

This gig she rigged up she called "Wagon *Anterior.*" Never, from a horse's point of view, had a vehicle been constructed with less consideration. The whole crazy business was backside to.

"Giddiap!" called Dorcas, as offensively as possible.

That "Giddiap!" for Thidwick was the very last straw.

He saw red. He saw orange. He saw green, blue and violet.
Something in Thidwick virtually exploded.

In the greatest horse-and-tree conflict that Coventry has ever
known, Dorcas J. Godiva discovered Horse Truth Number Two.
"Don't," was its substance, *"put the cart before the horse."*

Her wedding, however, was postponed for some time. It took more than five months to remove enough splinters to make the Lady of Research reasonably safe for Peeping Dick.

Arabella Godiva

IF ever a horse had reason to take to drink, it was Brutus. Arabella was wearing the poor devil down. So anxious was she to wed Peeping Harry that, even while she slept, she worked the horse like mad.

Nightly she would sleep-walk down to the stables, and all night she would sleep-trot over the hills.

Brutus, of course, cracked under the strain. Somehow he had learned that the fermented mash at the bottom of the silo had a soothing, consoling effect upon troubles. So, whenever he got the chance, he'd tip-hoof stealthily around to the silo and indulge himself in a little quiet lapping.

In no time at all, Brutus had degenerated into a drunken bum.

"Look at him, *look at him!*" cried Arabella one morning.

Brutus was suffering the most extravagant hangover ever experienced by man or by beast. He lay sprawled on his rumpled straw, his eyes bloodshot, his nostrils aquiver. His addled head swam, devoid of all horse sense. As a colleague in science he was no help at all.

"He's a drunk!" said Arabella. "And I want another horse."

But Hedwig spoke up sharply. "Arabella, I've known Brutus since he was a colt—so high. What Brutus is today, you yourself have made him. You'll stick to him through thick and through thin! Come along, girls." Arabella's sisters stalked out of the barn.

Arabella frowned down at old besotted Brutus. Through this dissipated hulk lay her only road to freedom. Brutus, she realized, would have to be reformed.

"Oh, for goodness sake," she snapped, "make a horse of yourself!" She tugged at his halter.

Slowly, painfully, he staggered to his feet. He swayed there, weaving, on four legs of rubber. Through the open window, he caught a glimpse of the silo. His murky eyes brightened.

"Oh, no, you don't!" shouted Arabella. And she dragged the poor creature straight out to the pump.

"Pump stuff!" shuddered Brutus. "I'll die before I touch it."
He did.

Arabella phrased her Horse Truth in the Oath Book very neatly:
"You can lead a horse to water, but you can't make him drink."

Then, underneath, she scribbled in a big conceited scrawl: "By the time you old maids read this, I'll be Mrs. Peeping Harry."

Mitzi Godiva

"*Mitzi, my Sweet,*" wrote Able-bodied Seaman Peeping Jack, from his perch in the crow's-nest of the *Bouncing Queen Maeve,* plying the trade routes of Ultima Thule.

"It's seven years now. How about that Horse Truth?

"Your true-love,

"Peeping Jack."

He sealed the letter with a kiss and posted it the next week in the port of Bru Na Boinn. From Bru Na Boinn to Cuin Selinn to Brenig Lag to Thwil-on-Thyne, by sea-skiff post and ox-drawn dray, the love note came to Coventry.

It reached Mitzi in the stable on Midsummer's Day, that dreadfully hot August of 1073.

As she read the brisk fresh words, Mitzi was transported. The stables, the horses—all drifted away. . . . She heard the shrill pipe of sea gulls, felt the tang of salt spray. The surge of mighty rollers roared in her ears. She thought of lobsters and clams. . . . Mitzi Godiva was a true sailor's sweetheart.

The vision faded. . . . Once more to her nostrils came the smell of mildewed straw. Mitzi Godiva was back in the barn. Horses! Stupid hay-munching beasts of dry land! If only they were sea horses; that would be different!

"Sea horses. . . ." mused Mitzi. "A glorious idea. I shall go at the horse from the nautical angle."

In a giddy frenzy of excitement, she plunged into the problems of equestrian aquatics. She swam horses across ponds and she swam them in harbors. She dived them from chalk cliffs and she fed them on seaweed.

When her horses had become thoroughly at home in the water, Mitzi was ready for her Great Experiment.

She designed and constructed a horse-propelled rowboat. And she named it the *Peeping Jack,* in honor of her sweetheart.

It was a beautiful thing, far ahead of its time, and, generally speaking, it worked like a charm.

It was not the lack of sea-horsepower that made the craft a failure. It was the hammer, hammer, hammer on the hard oak treads. When every voyage was halfway through, the horse came down with Hoof Burn.

The *Peeping Jack* was a one-way cruiser. Mitzi sank it and faced the whole problem anew.

One blustery day in the following March, Mitzi slipped moorings and headed up the river in the *Peeping Jack II*, Mitzi at the tiller, Clover on the treadmill, and Dapples, the spare mare, perched high in the poop.

Against a stiff swirling current, Clover pushed on. In three hours, she clocked off a good thirteen knots. Then she stopped. It was Hoof Burn.

"Dapples," commanded Mitzi, smiling and confident, "take your trick on the treadmill. Climb down and go forward."

It was a wonderful scheme and it ought to have worked.

And it would have, if Dapples had followed Mitzi's instructions. But instead of passing sideways, according to plan, Dapples attempted to go *over* Clover.

A most disastrous piece of horseplay ensued.

The wreckage of the *Peeping Jack II* was swept down the river. No one ever saw what happened to the horses, but her sisters saw Mitzi as she bounced down the rapids, clinging to some flotsam, headed hell-bent for sea.

"Here's one for the book," her voice came back in anguish. *"Never change horses in the middle of the stream."*

Several days later, she was picked up off Guernsey, oddly enough, by the *Bouncing Queen Maeve*. And the sailor who saved her was good Peeping Jack.

They were married at sea by the captain.

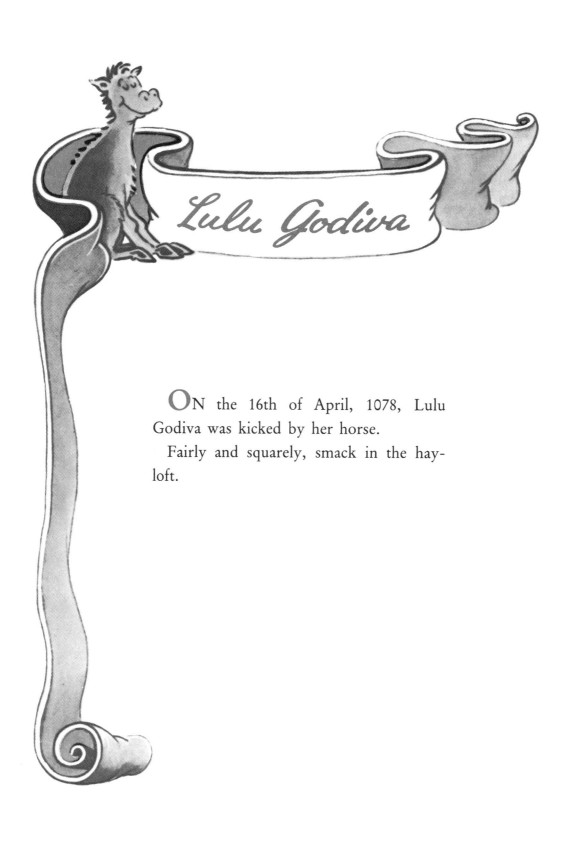

Lulu Godiva

ON the 16th of April, 1078, Lulu Godiva was kicked by her horse.

Fairly and squarely, smack in the hayloft.

In the hay, to her amazement, she found Peeping Drexel's diamond stickpin. He had lost it there, a-trysting, on a previous occasion.

Thus Lulu discovered that *horseshoes are lucky.*

Lulu Godiva made a beeline for the Oath Book. She jotted down her Horse Truth and left the place forever.

Gussie Godiva

THE Sisters Godiva had dwindled to two. Ten winters had passed since Lulu had wed Drexel. Gussie and Hedwig were still deep in toil, fruitlessly groping for Truths in the stables.

Hedwig Godiva, placid and hopeful, faced each day with new patience and faith. But Gussie took to thinking too much about love. Repressed, she smoldered with passions galore.

Each night she dreamed dreams unbecoming a maiden. Awaking in anguish, she would light a taper and brood the night through, staring at the portrait of Peeping Sylvester.

"Come to me, loved one," his likeness would whisper. "Come to me, sweet, and the hell with your oath!"

"Dear handsome," she would sigh, "if only I dared."

In 1091, just three nights before Michaelmas, Gussie gave in to her turbulent urge. She tore up her bedclothes to make an escape rope and lowered herself furtively from her high turret window. It was the night of Peeping Sylvester's birthday. Oath or no oath, she was going to surprise him.

As it worked out, however, she surprised only Hedwig, who was a very light sleeper.

"You climb," snapped Hedwig, "straight back up those bed sheets! And from now on, young lady, you'll be watched every minute."

More frustrated than ever, poor Gussie climbed back. To elude the sharp eye of Hedwig, she realized, was impossible. There were no two ways about it. *She would have to find a Horse Truth.*

She cudgeled her brains as she never had before. Her mind galloped wild along the most amazing thought-lanes.

By dawn she had her Horse Truth—a strange one, perhaps, but entirely legitimate.

Hedwig, spying from a wagon, saw Gussie approaching. Eyes ablaze, she swept on toward the stables. She clutched a mysterious bundle tight to her breast. Hair streaming behind her, Gussie vanished inside. The ancient barn door shut behind her with a slam.

For a moment—breathless silence. Hedwig strained hard to hear. Through the walls came the sudden sounds of commotion. The crinkle and the crackle of wrapping paper ripping . . . the uneasy scuffle of a score of nervous hoofs.

A splashing of liquids! A terrified whinny!

The door of the stable burst wide open!

Out into the world hurtled Gussie Godiva, clinging to the back of a screaming mad nag, painted forelock to fetlock a dizzy blue-green!

"That," she was shrieking, "is my contribution! *That is a horse of another color!*"

As she streaked down the road, like a lunatic comet, the giddiest
Godiva broke into song. The staid hills of Coventry blushed as they
heard her, bawdy and raucous and badly off-key:

> *"High diddle dester*
> *Ho, diddle dum,*
> *Peeping Sylvester,*
> *Here I come."*

Hedwig Godiva

NEITHER Hedwig nor Peeping Frelinghuysen was getting any younger. At seventy he had lost his job teaching harp at the county day school. When his fingers had stiffened, the school board let him go.

"Now I can spend my whole time," he wrote Hedwig, "making plans for our marriage." Every warm day the faithful old lover would pack up his basket and trudge with his dog to the top of the hill. There he would lie all day long in the sunshine, gazing far away at the Castle Godiva.

Its turrets still rose high, but no longer quite so proudly. Here and there a crumbling battlement had fallen into the moat. The bell in the watch tower was muted with fungus. Everywhere grew blackthorn, sourgrass and nink.

The Castle Godiva was going to pot.

With her bed and her bureau, Hedwig had long ago moved into the barn. Each day her situation was growing more critical. Time had been taking its toll in the stables.

On December 31, 1105, she was down to her very last horse, Parsifal. And the poor antique gelding was at death's door with the grippe. Yet, without frenzy, without panic, Hedwig attended the failing steed's needs, dosing him hourly with bowls of hot hippocrass, bundling him on the half hour in newly warmed straw.

As the old year was dying, Parsifal seemed just a little stronger. Hedwig, for the tonic effect it might have on his spirits, got out her horn and blew the New Year in. It was not just a blast that she blew, but a prayer. The hopes of a lifetime went into that horn. And something within Parsifal responded to the call.

Hedwig finally went to bed, smiling. She had pulled him through his crisis. Parsifal would live.

He did live, but Hedwig never saw him again. While she lay deep in the sleep of exhaustion, horse thieves stealthily broke in.

An hour before dawn, Hedwig woke with a start. Parsifal's box stall was empty. Her last horse was gone!

Any other woman would have dissolved into tears.

But Hedwig Godiva was not that kind. From the depths of an impossible situation, she rose to pluck a Horse Truth out of thin air.

"Don't," she exclaimed as she went out and did it, *"lock the barn door after the horse has been stolen!"*

The stars over Coventry winked as they watched her. With her age-mellowed bridal veil crammed in a satchel, she plunged, humming, through the snowdrifts to the cottage of her ever-patient Peeping.